Nature never ceases to reinvent itself. Its imagination simply knows no limits as it regenerates and strengthens through diversity and multiplicity.

to Flavia & Bárbara

The Book of IMPRUDENT FLORA

Claudio Romo

Translation by David Haughton

GINGKO PRESS

A travel diary written by Lázaro de Sahagún,
eminent naturalist and explorer

My name is Lázaro de Sahagún. I am an explorer, and I study the astonishing repertoire of forms through which life expresses itself. I travel the world on board my herbarium ship, The Green Cabinet, where I gather, catalogue and preserve nature's formidable creative verve and its strangest fruits.

The illustrated travelogue you are reading recounts the botanical discoveries I made on the Specular Isle, a remote piece of land lost in the Pacific Ocean somewhere between Tierra del Fuego and Antarctica. This vegetal bestiary is subdivided into ten sections, each devoted to a particular plant, every one of which is notable for the indomitably bizarre characteristics which underlie its role as a prodigious ambassador of nature's vivacity.

We set sail from the port of Valparaíso in the spring of 1868, navigating towards the South Pole. The mission's goal was to investigate the ghostly wandering islands of ice sighted by whaling boats plying the remote routes far south of South America.

After five weeks of tranquil navigation, disturbed only by impetuous gusts of wind off the Gulf of Penas, we had left Tierra del Fuego far astern.

While we were proudly ploughing through the seas that separate the American continent from Antarctica, in the middle of the Drake Passage, near Elephant Island, one day our ship plunged into prodigiously thick banks of fog… a decidedly unusual phenomenon for those latitudes. At the same time, the water surrounding our vessel underwent a rapid thickening process, until it became so dense that no further progress was possible. And yet — however strange this may seem — we continued to move, while also observing that the ship's compass continuously indicated abrupt and apparently random shifts of direction.

It seemed as though we had penetrated inside a gigantic capsule of climatic alteration, where neither day nor night existed, and where a curtain of burnished light with greenish and ochre shadings wound around us unceasingly. At one point, overcome by desperation, we lowered our lifeboats, but the density of the water — whose consistency verged upon that of the stickiest gum arabic — precluded the slightest movement.

Having spent about a month in this condition of absolute isolation, when everyone felt themselves on the verge of sliding into madness, the phenomenon abruptly disappeared, revealing nearby the most extraordinary island any of us had ever seen.

We named it Specular Isle, because its landscape — in any part of the island, and observed from any point of view — invariably appeared to the viewer as perfectly symmetrical: every detail observed to one's left-hand side was a perfect mirror-image of every detail observed to one's right-hand side, and vice versa. Consequently, when the sun rose in the east at dawn, in the same instant a perfect copy rose on the horizon to the west. Likewise at sunset. Only on the stroke of midday would the sun for a moment become a single body.

The Patagonian Colossus

The second day after disembarking, however, we noticed that the symmetry of the landscape had begun to diminish somewhat (without us having found a shred of explanation for the phenomenon).

As our first task, we began to analyse the seaweed on the island's coastline. We were diligently engaged in this activity when we suddenly found ourselves face to face with the colossal figure of a person whose height must have measured roughly twenty metres. After taking one look at this apparition, we fled towards the sea. However, we soon recovered from our initial shock (the giant had meanwhile delicately plucked us up from the water with his fingers), as we realised how polite and well-behaved he was, how curious he was about us, and how pleased he was to answer our questions.

Our friend – the sound of whose name reminded us of the crackle of fire caused by burning dried quila[1] – belonged to a community of invisible whale-riders. Apparently, the two species are branches of the same broad family, and therefore share distant family ties.

The ability to make themselves invisible, our giant companion explained, had developed from a very ancient hunting strategy involving body painting using pigments extracted from seaweed and roots. These endowed their bodies with a permanent bluish hue that made them invisible unless observed from less than four metres away, and only on bright sunny days.

Since his community suffered direly during the intense cold of winter in those climes, at the first sign of autumn the giant's duty was to set off and chase the sun in its long journey northwards, following the dark and icy tracks it left in its wake. He then ritually captured the sun, using enormous ropes made of wind which every morning fettered down the blazing orb and prevented it from abandoning the invisible whale-riders' mysterious territory.

That evening, before our group set off, the amicable colossus gently placed me on top of his head, so that I could admire the surrounding panorama: the whole island stretched away before my eyes, vast, marvellous and bristling with abundant vegetation.

While I was up there, a dense cloud of butterflies enveloped us totally.

Specular Ambrosia

This plant, or certainly part of it, is of a ghostly nature. No one has ever succeeded in touching one, or in seeing a solitary exemplar, since it only manifests itself in groups. This suggests the following hypothesis: if Ambrosia genuinely exists, there must be only one authentic exemplar, which never dies and is never born. All the others are simply reflections of this one blueprint, generated with the express purpose of protecting it by distracting attention from the real thing.

If someone approaches a field of Ambrosia, they are confronted by a spectral and kaleidoscopically symmetric vision, as in a valley of mirrors. The plants on the periphery are diaphanous and evanescent in appearance, while those near the centre flaunt bright red or blue colours. But if the visitor tries to reach the central part, hoping to grasp the one real plant, a dramatic and dizzying process of specular multiplication is set in motion that confuses them and leaves them dazed and disorientated.

The name Ambrosia is derived from its exquisite aroma, evocative of lavender and lemon balm. It is said that at the centre of the corolla nestles a vegetal mirror, in which it is possible to contemplate one's authentic hidden face.

Peregrine Aloysia

It is said that this plant produces a single fruit, not unlike a strawberry, and extremely delicious. However, if its fruit is plucked, the plant dies instantly – a peculiarity which long ago brought the species to the brink of extinction.

Fortunately, the ingenious Aloysia was by no means resigned to annihilation at the hands of those who wished to steal its fruit, and consequently developed a first line of defence that consisted of a fearsome armour of thorns. Regrettably, however, both men and animals developed ways of penetrating this defence, and the species again came close to extinction.

A second defensive strategy involved the development of eight protrusions from the fruit, resembling the hairy legs of a ghastly spider. But once again, both men and animals learned to ignore this bluff and continued gorging themselves thoughtlessly on the delicious fruit. However, enough of the species survived to metamorphosise their roots into a pair of sturdy claw-like feet. This enabled the plants – as soon as any threat of a fruit-eater appeared – to scurry quickly to a place of safety. Thanks to this evolutionary tactic, the species has survived down to the present day and specimens are now numbered in their thousands.

In the opposite illustration, a mature Aloysia is observing me prudently while drinking from a small lake.

Cayetana Transfigured

Describing Cayetana is not a simple operation, especially since its form and structure are in constant mutation.

A plausible explanation is that originally the vulnerable Cayetana, lacking defences such as prickles or poison, exploited its transformative abilities to mimic the characteristics of thorny, poisonous or stinging plants, such as the nettle or the litre[2]. Subsequently, realising the infinite potential of its gift, the plant opted to transcend such simple mimetic tactics, abandoning itself with relish to celebrating its imaginative genius, reinventing itself continually in a dizzying vegetal kaleidoscope.

According to my observations, Cayetana passes through 240 different transformative phases every day. In order to understand this behaviour, I catalogued these phases into four main cycles: night, dawn, afternoon, and dusk.

Night: while asleep, Cayetana assumes every possible shade of blue, while its texture resembles that of a damp cloth, or the scales of certain fish. Its shapes are as geometric as minerals, and its body becomes as shiny and transparent as quartz. Its perfume shifts between mint and rue.

Dawn: Cayetana welcomes each new day by generating dozens of small tentacle-shaped petals, arranged in concentric circles. During this phase, its coloration shifts through every shade of yellow and red, including luminous ochre hues. At around 10 a.m., it emanates an intense golden light which dazzles anyone in the vicinity.

Afternoon: after midday, Cayetana moves through hues of bright but transparent yellow, while to the touch it becomes softer, with an almost colloidal texture, to the point where one can push a finger through it. Its bodily consistency resembles that of a jellyfish.

Dusk: between 6 and 10 p.m., Cayetana grows astonishingly, reaching up to thirty metres high. In this phase, it takes on shapes that seem to echo the bizarre vegetal fantasies displayed by Hieronymus Bosch in the central panel of his Garden of Earthly Delights.

Levitating Amelia

Exemplars of this small plant – as numerous as grains of sand – swarm in the sky above the beaches of the northern coast of the island, where they feed on cochayuyo[3], the most delicious seaweed in the world.

On sighting this species, we approached them for study purposes, but as soon as they perceived our presence they extruded thin butterfly tongues from their many mouths (between ten and fifteen), which they then used to lick or caress our hands and faces. We woke up from a series of confused dreams roughly five hours later, deducing that Amelia's saliva contains a notably effective narcotic substance. The plant's body might best be described as resembling a strange mixture between the wings of a moth and the branches of a peach tree.

In November and January, Amelia disappears underground in order to mature its three fruits, which appear as minute buds of flowering wings.

Coloane[4] – one of our sailors – was extremely fond of Amelias, because he was convinced they had the ability to sooth his chronic headaches.

Colossal Cassiopea

Cassiopea is a kind of giant cactus, not unlike the agave, but with a reddish colouration. Its most notable feature is its ability – whenever confronted by any kind of threat – to launch its needles with extraordinary power: each of these resembles a javelin from one to three metres in length and weighing roughly five kilos.

In past centuries, Cassiopea was used as an assault weapon against castles and walled towns, alongside the catapults and ballistae of the period. Positioned on top of special large carts, and provoked by fire-torches, this species acted as a deadly military weapon.

In time, however, its military use was reduced, partly because the random victims of its lethal spears were evenly divided between the troops of both armies, and partly because the development of guns and cannons rendered this weapon of mass destruction increasingly obsolete.

Anyone trying to cross a field of Cassiopeas is in tremendous danger, since the slightest disturbance of the plants would be likely to leave them instantly and multiply impaled – a fact confirmed to me by the sight of a couple of human skeletons, run through by numerous deadly javelins.

The moist heart of the Cassiopea secretes a white sap which can be fermented to form an intense liquor with a taste similar to the Mexican pulque[5].

Flaming Calliope

According to early studies, this highly unusual plant "is born among fires, feeds on flames and creates a desert wherever it grows". The plant, whose leaves are actually small tongues of flame of variable density, never grows to more than two or three metres high… and yet a limited number of exemplars can reduce whole valleys to ash.

Documented accounts of Calliope stretch back to ancient times, and describe how exemplars of this flaming plant were always kept in the earliest human settlements. Subsequently, its dangerous instability – plus the discovery of less risky means of producing fire – caused it to be increasingly confined to places far away from inhabited areas. Calliope thus became a mythical plant, although the genuine article continued until recently to be used by artisans such as blacksmiths and potters, who grew it in great secrecy.

The name Calliope will have derived from the widespread belief that the plants are actually fragments from the star of the same name that fell to Earth many thousands of years ago, before the appearance of Homo sapiens, and which have burned ever since in the ardent hope of rejoining their celestial mother.

In the tenth century, the Sect of Penitent Judases, also known as The Supplicants, worshipped Calliope because they saw in these burning bushes "the furious hand of God", and preached that a hail of these plants would announce the beginning of the end of the world.

It is said that the heat generated by Calliope's flames is recommended for alleviating arthritic and lumbago pains, which prompted me to capture one, to eventually take home with me. Unfortunately, excited by the irregular movements of the waves, my hoped-for heat remedy set the boat on fire!

In the opposite illustration, I am examining a Calliope branch, protected by a diving suit.

Pandora the Anguisher

Pandora is a spectral plant which feeds on the suffering and anxiety surrounding it. In turn, its pale purplish emanations generate pain and despair in those nearby, and by night the wind among its branches causes moans of anguish which, to our astonishment, we could hear from aboard our ship. This was enough to sow the seeds of discord among our crew, while the most saturnine of them were assailed by such melancholy that they could barely contain their tears.

Pandora awakes after sunset, when its transparent petals open to receive the glow of the moon, which regulates its life-cycle.

In order to study and catalogue an exemplar, we had to make use of special containers and protective clothing, in order to remain immune to its desolate emanations.

Every time I approach it without the necessary protection, I am overwhelmed by the uselessness of my knowledge and the futility of my miserable projects.

Voracious Matilda

In his book A Journey in the Phantasmagorical Garden, *the erudite Apparitio Albinus – known as "the phytophile" – writes:*

> Matilda,
> flowering trap and heart-eater,
> image of pain and futile illusion of desire,
> you capture other lives and devour them.

Considered one of the five flowers of Limbo, since ancient times Matilda can be seen in collections and bestiaries of imaginary creatures, alongside gryphons, amphisbaenae, and basilisks.

Today we know that Matilda is a carnivorous plant whose flower secretes, at the end of its pistil, an ectoplasmic substance which gives shape to the appetites of its prey. What remains a mystery is how Matilda guesses what its victims desire to eat, or whether it is its victims who somehow influence the ectoplasmic substance which, as though in a kaleidoscope, offers all the possible forms of their deepest desires.

As an experiment, we placed a mouse in front of Matilda: immediately a crumb of cheese appeared in the centre of the flower, complete with a cheesy aroma. Subsequently, we placed Pussy – our ship's cat – in the same position, with the result that the flower displayed a mouse (about to eat a piece of cheese).

When we put a bird near Matilda, a small earthworm appeared inside the flower.

Bárbara Vegetalopolis

Every exemplar of this extraordinary tree is home to a city, or rather, a series of citadels. I could even go so far as to say that each tree contains a kind of nation, made up of various distinct but interrelated communities. These are inhabited by perfect but microscopic humanoids, which are visible only via a complex system of tiny mirrors.

Once these creatures had seen me, and overcome the agitation caused by my appearance in their territory, they sent their eldest citizen to speak to me as their ambassador. During our long conversation, I learned that these people descended from the crew members of a group of merchant ships which had fallen victim – just like us – to a totally dense fog in the Magellan Straight, and then finally reached this island, where their descendants have lived for three hundred years. According to the old man, their ancestors had come from a remote country called Portugal, which had been mythologised in his people's memory until it had assumed a status similar to the Garden of Eden for us.

Their change in dimension, the old man told me, had been caused by their habitual consumption of a fruit called "Lilliputian Strawberry", whose side effect was to shrink those who ate it. The addictive power of this fruit was such that, despite becoming aware of the disturbing transformation on their bodies, to this day they continue to feed upon it.

The old man then told me how, roughly two hundred years ago, their reduced stature had already made them easy prey for many kinds of animals (especially birds, their most deadly predators). This was when they made the decision to live among the dense branches of this mighty tree.

During the summer they live inside the tree's fruit, while in winter they take refuge inside its hollow branches. Their main activities are trading in lichen, hunting and training the insects that they fly on. If attacked by birds of prey, they form large swarms so tight they hide the sun. Their total number is extremely difficult to estimate, since they have never succeeded in carrying out a census, partly because they have totally lost contact with many communities.

After our farewell, I was escorted by a swarm of wasp-riders, one of which is depicted in the opposite illustration.

The Flower of the Cycle

In his Faithful Chronicle of the World That I Saw, Thaddaeus Squint wrote "Among the ancient peoples of Hindustan, the so-called 'Flower of the Cycle' was used in their annual purification rituals. At the sight of it, all the citizens totally lost their memories, and the priests then had the task of redistributing on a random basis all roles within the community…".

One day, as we were searching for an observation point for our topographic studies, we found ourselves near the summit of the island's highest hill. From here we observed from a distance the bright light coming from a strange flower. We set off towards it, curious to find out more and to study the plant's luminous properties, but before we could take any notes a dazzling white light surrounded us and totally blinded us. The light penetrated through our eyes and into our brains, causing us to lose consciousness…

After this, the only thing I can remember is that we returned to consciousness on a pier in the port of Valparaíso. None of us had preserved anything more than the vaguest memories of our journey. Little by little, we tried to reconstruct our adventure using the samples we had gathered, our notes and illustrations… but the mystery of our return to Valparaíso has ever since remained totally incomprehensible.

Many times have I tried to refocus my mind on that most arcane and disturbing flower, without ever succeeding, unfortunately. Presumably nature must have generated it in order to supply us with the possibility of cyclically liberating ourselves, after a certain period of time, of all our errors, of all our shame, and of the unbearable weight of our actions.

Epilogue

Retracing in thought the circumstances of our bizarrely mysterious voyage, the only hypothesis I can propose is this: if our planet is – as I believe – a living organism aware of its own existence, places like that island act as reserves, where the Earth preserves memories of its creations in order to safeguard life in future periods of global decadence. This means that the enigma of their geographical position combined with the awareness of their existence provides the key to the necessary perpetuation of life.

Lázaro de Sahagún
Valparaíso, 1868

The idea for The Book of Imprudent Flora came to me in Mexico, while I was illustrating the book El cuento de los contadores de cuentos[6] (The Tale of the Story Tellers). When I saw it published, I realized just how interesting it could be to publish illustrated books, and how much their communicative and expressive potential could be increased by mixing images and text. I was so enthusiastic about this that I decided to make the creation of this kind of book an essential part of my work, which until then had been focused on images alone (mostly engravings). When I returned to Chile in 2005, I began to work on Flora. I wanted it to be a catalogue, an inventory of items in an imaginary collection… because I love museums (especially museums of Natural History, History and Technology), but regretfully, Chile doesn't have many such museums. So I felt that Flora could constitute a portable museum. I wanted the book to appeal to young people, to introduce them to the magic of collections, of museums, of places where objects and their histories can be gathered, thus to create a dialogue between now and the past, and with literature and art. That way, Flora would become a meeting place and a treasure-trove of information and experience. And so I began to draw a vegetal bestiary, a book of imaginary botany.

I was strongly influenced by reading the short story Tlön, Uqbar, Orbis Tertius[7] and The Book of Imaginary Beings[8]. In the former, Borges conceives among other things a fictitious territory, while in the second he assembles a bestiary of fantastic beings that pervade Western and Eastern cultures. Both showed me what I could create with Flora.

Another fundamental influence was The Florentine Codex[9] by Brother Bernardino de Sahagún, which I had read during my specialist studies in Mexico and which bears witness to the way that pre-Hispanic graphic culture blended with the European narrative tradition. Organised like an encyclopaedia containing all the information gathered by Brother Bernardino in Mexico, the book is written in Spanish and Nahuatl[10], but being an illustrated book it speaks with three languages: drawings being capable of translating all the realities which make up the world into a single language.

The book – a place where different traditions and kinds of knowledge interact – is one of the objects that best represent the human race.

This is why in Flora the two forms of narration, the two arts of literature and drawing, interweave together to generate a single fabric: ourselves.

The Book of Imprudent Flora was first published in 2007 by the Chilean publisher Lom, with the title El álbum de la flora imprudente.

Claudio Romo

Notes

1. Quila: a perennial bamboo variety, widely present in South America, especially in Chile and Argentina.
2. Litre: a tree that thrives in Chile, whose leaves cause strong allergic skin reactions, including irritation, itching and blisters. It is said that the best way to avoid this allergy is to greet the tree politely with the words "Good day, Mr. Litre". It is also said, however, that insulting the tree – and preferably spitting at it – also reduces the likeliness of allergic reactions.
3. Cochayuyo: edible seaweed from South America, from the Quechuan *qhucha yuyu*, "sea plant".
4. Coloane: probably an ancestor of the more famous Francisco Coloane (1910-2002), a Chilean writer, traveller and sailor often compared to authors such as Herman Melville, Jules Verne and Joseph Conrad. Son of a captain of whaling ships, Francisco too carried out expeditions to various parts of the world, including the Antarctic, China and the Galapagos Islands, always filled with a profound sense of wonder at Nature's magnificence and its amazing variety. He wrote assiduously of his travels and his native country in various books, translated and published in many languages, including English.
5. Pulque: an alcoholic drink rich in mineral salts and nutrients, obtained through the fermentation of sap from the *Agave salmiana*, a succulent plant native to Mexico and widely spread across Central America since the age of the Aztec Empire, when it was used for religious rituals and considered as sacred. This liqueur has a milk-like appearance, with a viscous consistency and a bitter taste, and can be drunk neat or mixed with fruit juice.
6. *El cuento de los contadores de cuentos*, text by Nacer Khemir, illustrations by Claudio Romo, Fondo de Cultura Económica, 2004.
7. "Tlön, Uqbar, Orbis Tertius", in *Fictions*, Jorge Luis Borges, Penguin, 2000.
8. *The Book of Imaginary Beings*, Jorge Luis Borges, Viking, 2005; Vintage, 2002.
9. *Florentine Codex* (*Historia general de las cosas de Nueva España*), Bernardino de Sahagún (the codex is kept in the Biblioteca Medicea Laurenziana in Florence, Italy, and can be consulted online at www.wdl.org/10096).
10. Nahuatl: an Aztec language spoken in Mexico.

The books that inspired this work:

Florentine Codex
(*Historia general de las cosas de Nueva España*)
Bernardino de Sahagún

The Invention of Morel
Adolfo Bioy Casares
New York Review Books / Signature Books, 2003

The Book of Imaginary Beings
Jorge Luis Borges
Viking, 2005; Vintage, 2002

The Stowaway
Francisco Coloane
Maryland Books, 1964

A Journey in the Phantasmagorical Garden of Apparitio Albinus
Claudio Romo
#logosedizioni, 2016

Hieronymus Bosch. Complete Works
Stefan Fischer
Taschen, 2014

THE BOOK OF IMPRUDENT FLORA
© Claudio Andrés Salvador Francisco Romo Torres

First Published in the United States of America, 2017
by Gingko Press, Inc. - 1321 Fifth Street, Berkeley, CA 94710, USA
www.gingkopress.com

Under License from #logosedizioni

Originally Published in Italy by © #logosedizioni, 2017

Translation: David Haughton
Layout: Alessio Zanero

All rights reserved.
No part of this publication may be reproduced,
stored in a retrieval system, or transmitted in any form or
by any means, electronic, mechanical, photocopying, recording,
or otherwise, without the prior consent of the publisher.

ISBN: 978-1-58423-694-8
Printed in China by Book Partners China Ltd